KARNI ZEMEL

THE CARPET
OF SOLOMON

SULAMITH ISH-KISHOR
THE CARPET
OF SOLOMON

A Hebrew Legend

PICTURES BY URI SHULEVITZ

PANTHEON BOOKS

Library of Congress catalog card number: 65-20658

FOR GIDEON

who I believe still knows

I

The great King Solomon lay supported by silken cushions on his couch of ivory, under the tall palm trees of his royal gardens. Black slaves cooled the air about his head with fans of many-colored feathers. Around him were gathered the brilliantly robed courtiers, watching for the least change of expression in his face. Rows of helmeted soldiers, armed with spears, guarded the marble-mosaic terrace.

From his high-placed seat the Great King looked

down over his city of Jerusalem, which lay spread out below in a network of twisting, narrow streets, with groups of dull green cypress pointing upward among the flat, yellow-white roofs and the faintly tinted domes.

King Solomon turned to his favorite servant, the captain of the Royal Guard, who stood at his right hand, clothed in crimson, a plumed helmet on his erect head, and a chain of rare yellow rubies across his soldierly chest.

"Benaiah," said the King, "go to my inmost treasure chamber, to the hidden cabinet which you alone know of, and fetch my peerless emerald, through which I can see clearly for many miles. I will observe what is going on in the city of my people."

Bowing low, Benaiah hurried away. In a few minutes he was back, holding the marvelous jewel in his palm, where it blazed like a fragment of the sun. King Solomon leaned forward and took the emerald from the captain's hand. Resting on his elbow among the heaped-up cushions, he set the gem to his eye.

3

Through its polished lens the Great King distinguished with perfect clearness all the life of Jerusalem, even to the far-off roads beyond the triple walls.

In the brown shadows of the chief market place he made out the tiny white-clad figures of donkey drivers, goading their little, burdened animals among the opposing streams of buyers and sellers of wares. People in voluminous colored robes pushed and jostled in every direction. Before the stalls, decked out with well-displayed goods, men sat catching at the skirts of passers-by to make them stop and look at their offerings.

Foreign merchants unloaded their kneeling camels, shaking out rich silks and woven garments of dyed wool before the eyes of the natives. Small groups intent on business formed close around each merchant, bargaining, with restless waving of hands and active nodding of heads, for brocades, for tropical birds as bright as rainbows, for lively black apes, or for long tusks of yellow ivory, while the water sellers lowered their bulging goatskin bottles from their ragged shoulders to give the merchants a drink.

4

As he gazed with interest through the clear, powerful lens of the emerald, the Great King's eye was held by a strange incident.

Into the market place slowly came a merchant, leading a camel that limped on one foot as though it had traveled far. The merchant halted, made the camel kneel, and unbound from between its humps a roll of carpet.

Loosening part of the fabric, which the King observed to be of strange design and marvelous hues, the merchant shook it out and exposed it to view. At once all passers-by stopped. They crowded around the carpet, touching it, turning its corners this way and that, examining the underside, rubbing the texture between their fingers, and finally shaking their heads in wonder. The merchant was speaking with grave and solemn gestures, while every moment the throng increased, until it was impossible for anyone to get by.

The Great King marveled as he watched. Surely this was no ordinary carpet! Even as he looked there was a backward movement in the crowd; all heads

6

turned away, the throng dissolved, and the merchant stood unnoticed next to his camel, onto whose back he slowly proceeded to refasten the carpet.

King Solomon's curiosity rose high. He stroked his pearl-braided beard, frowned, and put down the emerald. With a nod he summoned a guard.

"In the chief market place you will find a merchant putting away a carpet which no one will buy. Go, bring him here."

With a clash of arms the guard saluted and hastened off. Raising the jewel again to his eye, the Great King saw the guard enter the market place, talk to the frightened merchant, and lead him away with his carpet. A few minutes later the guard again entered the King's presence, followed by a short, black-bearded man in a travel-stained robe, who carried in his arms a rolled-up carpet.

"Have no fear," said Solomon kindly. "Only those who do wrong need fear me, for I can penetrate their very thoughts. What is this carpet which you carry?"

"Most glorious and powerful King, wisest of man-

kind!" stammered the merchant. "It is a magic carpet. It is woven with the name of God. It has powers unknown in any other carpet. Whoever sits upon this carpet may command it to transport him any-where in the world, and it will at once obey. There is nothing like it under Heaven."

"And yet no one wanted to buy it?" said the King, fixing his calm eyes on the merchant.

"Most mighty King, the price is sixty thousand pieces of gold!"

"If it is so wonderful a treasure, it may well command so high a price. Show it to me!"

The merchant bowed his turbaned head to the ground; setting the carpet down, he hastily unrolled it. Solomon leaned his crowned head forward to see.

The fabric was woven with strange designs and inscriptions in various unknown tongues. The King's eyes gleamed and his lips moved silently as he read the inscriptions, for he knew all human languages, also the languages of birds, beasts, and demons.

Suddenly the King turned pale and a cry escaped

him. The courtiers rushed toward him in dismay, but with a wave of his hand the Great King dismissed them all from his presence, save only Benaiah and the merchant.

As soon as the rest had departed, he turned to the man and exclaimed sternly, "Tell me truthfully, as you value your life, where did you get this carpet?"

"O mighty King, I beseech you, be not angry with your slave! I received this carpet in a strange fashion. I was traveling through the desert with a camel-load of dates and figs from Smyrna. I had already arrived within the shadow of the black mountain when I was aware of a rushing sound beneath me. Soon I heard a great voice rumbling underneath the ground; it cried out, 'Merchant, deliver me, and I will give you a precious gift!' Terrified, I was about to flee from the spot when the voice began again: 'I swear by the Almighty Name that I will not harm you! Only lift up the stone which is beneath your feet, and I will make you the possessor of sixty thousand pieces of gold!' The thought of owning such wealth dazzled me. I asked no more questions, but looked down in the sand, where I made out the shape of a huge stone with a brass ring in it. I tucked up my garments, bent both my knees, took the ring in both hands and pulled with all my might. The sweat poured off my brows like water; my muscles felt as if they were being torn out. Still the voice beneath encouraged me to pull harder. The stone resisted as if it were a living thing clutching the earth. But at last, with a final, mighty effort, I tore it loose and jumped aside.

"A heavy black smoke flashing with red sparks rolled up out of the hole in the earth. The dreadful voice, now ten times louder than before, burst out exultingly, 'Free! Free! Merchant, I thank thee! Take this magic carpet. It will transport its owner to any place in the world in the twinkling of an eye. Sell it for sixty thousand pieces of gold, neither more nor less, according to our compact.'

"The smoke rolled away into the sky, became a thick, small cloud, and then disappeared. The air

cleared, and at my feet I found this carpet. I tested
it by ordering it to carry me to my home and back
again, which it did in a moment. This, O most
gracious King, is the true story! Be not wroth with
me, I pray you. I meant only to make my family
rich and to do a service to one in need."

The Great King's eyes glittered with eagerness.
Leaning forward, he took up a corner of the carpet
in his own hand and scrutinized it intently.

"It is as I thought! He who gave you this miraculous
carpet was Ashmodai, King of the Demons, and none
other. Go, bid my treasurer give you the sixty thousand pieces, and a bowlful of new pearls therewith."

The delighted merchant prostrated himself, utter-
ing cries of gratitude, and scurried off.

King Solomon arose and paced the marble mosaic
of the terrace, his handsome face burning with excite-
ment.

"Benaiah, this is the carpet which I have desired for
years! Wisest of men I am, and richest of kings. But
now I shall become the very King of kings! By means

of this carpet, I shall know what is going on from one end of the earth to the other. Nothing shall be hidden from me. I shall rule the whole world! I shall be"—he paused, looking full at Benaiah, his eyes alight—"I shall be like God!"

The captain's face turned white as ash beneath his brazen helmet.

"My lord!" he stammered. "Think what you are saying! Is not the eye of God upon you even now? This is blasphemy which you have uttered!"

Solomon stepped back and gazed in angry amazement at his captain.

"Dost thou tell *me* what I may say and what I may not say? Do I not read the souls of all men, and is there any earthly wisdom hidden from me? When I ride upon that carpet, shall not I be more than human?"

With horror and fear in his eyes, Benaiah looked down at the beautiful, misty colors and wondrous intertwining pattern of the carpet.

"Hear me, my lord King! This carpet is evil—the archdemon Ashmodai has sent this work of his hands to do you harm. Already it has caused you to speak evil words, which I fear the Lord God will punish. Hear the words of one who loves you, and cause this evil thing to be destroyed!"

As Benaiah uncrossed his muscular arms from his chest and stooped to pick up the carpet, prepared to fling it over the parapet, a moment's doubt entered Solomon's heart, and he hesitated. But the carpet began to glow with such mysterious, rich colors, and the strange words seemed to gaze at him with so many meanings, that he determined it must be his, come what would. He stepped forward and raised his hand in command. Benaiah slowly let the carpet down on the terrace and turned away in despair.

But the Great King walked slowly and triumphantly onto the crumpled folds and cried out:

"Carry me to the ends of the earth!"

Before Benaiah could fully turn around there was emptiness in the place where the King had been. Far up in the darkening blue of the hot sky a tiny speck was swiftly flying. In another moment it was gone.

15

II

While the captain's faithful heart was torn with fear, the heart of the Great King was thrilled with joy. Fast flew the magic carpet over hill and plain, over red desert and gray mountains, over wild lakes and jagged rocks, where the green sea foamed in the crooked inlets.

Never before had Solomon experienced so glorious, so grandly exhilarating a sensation. To see all the world rushing by beneath his eyes! Rising higher as it skimmed a lofty peak, the carpet dashed through chill clouds and clammy mists that hid earth and sky; it cleft through storms of black, whirling wind and sailed across abysses of cold, clear sunlight.

Never had the Great King felt so near to Heaven, and to the wisdom which God alone possesses. It seemed to him that he flew by his own power, and that the whole world and sky were his own. The fierce winds driving past him sang like the deep trumpets of heavenly heralds as they blew out his streaming garments. The rushing clouds dipped and bowed before him; the clear blaze of red light from the sun brightened the airy way before his feet. Undreamed-of knowledge came into his mind; he had visions of wisdom such as no other mortal could conceive. Like the wings of an angel he spread out his arms and cried:

"What difference is there now between me and God as He flies through His heavens? All wisdom is mine. I am as God Himself!"

In mid-air the carpet stopped.

The far clouds on the horizon lurched forward and fell suddenly away. The sky whirled about Solomon's head; he rocked, grew dizzy, and fell on his face on the carpet. When he sat up and opened his eyes, he could see nothing. He was in the midst of black darkness. Not even the tiny glimmer of a lonely star could he see.

He became aware that the carpet was mounting up and up at a terrific speed. Far down in the pit of dark beneath, the moon, a pale blue bubble, was visible. Soon that, too, vanished.

Still as death was the universe. Beyond all worlds he passed.

The chill of unearthly terror was in Solomon's heart. He drew his thin silken garments closer about his shuddering body. What was he to do? Ah! He would pray—pray to the God who had never denied his prayers. But although his lips opened, not a word of prayer came to his mind; he could not remember so much as the Name of God.

Horror froze him. His hair rose and his heart almost

19

stopped. With a strong effort of will he controlled his fear. He set his lips tight and lifted his head proudly, alone in that vast, wild darkness.

"I am the Great King," he said.

By this time the carpet was again descending. It sank rapidly down and down, dropping through floods of stars that glittered like the spearheads of an invisible army, falling down and still down, until it floated into the gray light of a wintry afternoon. Now it flew onward.

Shapes of grotesque mountains, changing outlines of withered countrysides flitted by in blurred glimpses. The carpet was slowing down. The Great King saw wide mountaintops below him; he distinguished dark specks of pine clusters down the sides of the grim ravines. Eagles, like living black dots, circled against the snowy caps of the mountain peaks.

On the side of a bleak crag the magic carpet came to rest. For a while King Solomon remained still, then slowly stretching his cramped limbs, he stood up painfully and gazed about him. Over his head, bare mountains curved threateningly inward, closing him in from the sky; at his feet the cliff gradually sloped, then dropped away suddenly, forming an abyss. Not a living thing was in sight, save only the eagles rising out of their nests below and disappearing again with a rustle of black wings in the stillness.

The King stepped off the carpet and walked a few paces forward. The abyss was almost at his feet. He made a step backward, half inclined to return to the carpet. But when he looked toward the place where he had left it, he saw with a thrill of terror that it had disappeared!

What was to be done now? He was left alone on the dismal mountain, unable to move, unable to return. He stood, biting his lips in distress. He could not remain where he was. He could not go forward or backward. He decided to climb the face of the mountain and see where it would lead him.

The rocky, upward slope was so steep that the King was forced to clutch at every projection in order not to lose his balance. His face flushed; he breathed hard;

his heart beat heavily with the unaccustomed exertion.
His feet, in their fine sandals of gilded leather, began
to blister. His white hands, laden with mystic rings
and gems of unknown value, were scratched and
bleeding, and his long, delicate fingernails were full
of grit and dirt.

In a fit of disgust, the King stopped climbing and
sat down upon a rock to consider. He shook the dirt
from his splendid garments and rubbed his dusty
hands in an effort to clean them. Involuntarily he
glanced about him as if he expected his servants to
come to his aid. He longed for Benaiah's presence.
But no—he was all alone on a barren crag at the end
of the world.

Would he have to spend the coming night upon the
open mountainside?

He looked up into the sky, already dim with the
approach of evening. Then he saw, through the mists
that trailed about the hidden mountaintop, the keen
gray glimmer of a cluster of steel-like towers. Circle
beyond circle, sharp as needles, they rose into the sky,

until the King's straining eyes could perceive only the glinting white specks of windows receding into the heights of air.

A square-shaped gleam, like the reflection of a huge mirror, began to play upon the clouds; the grumbling of faraway thunder made the air quiver, and a strong, cold wind swept round the mountainside. The King started to his feet. Fearing lest the storm should come upon him while he was still without shelter, he decided to climb as quickly as possible to the castle.

Heavy drops of rain were already falling on the King's face by the time he reached the walls of the palace. He looked for the door, but there was none to be seen. He moved slowly along the wall, expecting as he approached each bastion that there would be a door on the other side. But he could not find so much as a crack in the solid, smooth stone. He dragged his heavy feet on and on past countless bastions, with their interspaces of bare wall. The castle had no doors.

King Solomon at last stood still and knitted his brows. There was nothing to do but climb these difficult walls and force an entry into the castle through one of the windows. To creep like a beggar or a robber into a castle where he should have been received in kingly state hurt his royal dignity, but he did not doubt that, once inside, he would be treated with all the reverence due to the mightiest and wisest of kings.

Gripping the walls firmly with his bare, soft hands, he pulled himself up laboriously, catching at the few perilous projections. His garments tore at every step, his palms were cruelly bruised, his brows ached with weariness within the golden rim of his heavy crown.

The window ledge was reached at last; he sat down to breathe and compose himself before smashing the window, so as to be prepared with an answer of proper dignity when people came and demanded to know who he was.

He wrapped his fist in a fold of his satin robe and drove it into the glass. The pain nearly paralyzed his hand and bloodstains appeared through the blue material. But when King Solomon prepared to put his

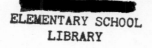
25

arm through the break he had made, his hand en-countered a smooth, unbroken surface of glass. The pane had become whole again!

A shudder passed over him and he wiped the sweat from his brow with his diamond-embroidered sleeve. At last the Great King realized that he was face to face with a force mightier than his own.

What was he to do? To what power could he appeal? Something struggled in his memory; he tried in vain to recall a Name—an Almighty Name—but he could not bring it to mind.

A heavy shadow falling over the mountain surprised the troubled King. There was a rustling like a forest of dry branches resisting a strong wind. Solomon looked up in fright. Hovering above him, on broad-spread wings that obscured a third of the sky, was a huge eagle. Solomon clung, dizzy, to his small, lonely window ledge far up on the side of the tower, and waited grimly for death.

But the eagle did not attempt to attack him.

"Ho, ho!" it croaked, and its voice was like a shower

of stones. "Who may this be, and what does he desire here at the end of the world, in the Palace of Eagles?"

Hope flashed back into Solomon's heart when the eagle spoke, and he exclaimed earnestly:

"I am the Great King. Take me up in your beak and carry me back to my country! Your reward shall be whatever you choose!"

Ruffling its plumes the eagle flew up to a higher tower.

"Oho! The Great King!" it cackled. "But you are the one who flies without wings! Who am *I* to carry *you?*" And it vanished into the tower, leaving King Solomon all alone between sky and earth.

The King was panic-stricken at this unexpected turn of affairs.

"Wait, wait!" he cried. Regardless of his broken fingernails and blistering knees, he seized the wall and heaved himself farther and farther up its height. Climbing madly, he reached another row of towers, where he was forced to rest, gasping, in a ledge formed by two adjoining buttresses.

He rested, and shut his eyes, for it turned him sick even to glance down into the bottomless chasms that opened in the rain like hungry, wet, black mouths.

Through his closed lids he sensed a heavy shadow. He opened them hastily, and looking up, saw a second eagle hovering above him, so large that its outspread wings obscured more than half the sky. It was old, very old; its eyes blinked continually and its scraggy feathers were dropping off with age.

In tones of anguish Solomon cried out, "I am the King of Israel—the Great King—Solomon, the son of David! Save me! Carry me back to my own country and your reward shall be anything you desire."

The eagle wearily flapped its old wings and the wind it made was so strong that the King had to cling tight to the ledge in order not to be blown away. Then it answered him in a voice like the thin roar of the breakers at sea.

"My desire is for eternal youth! Canst thou grant me that, King of Mortals? Then I will have strength to carry thee back to Israel!"

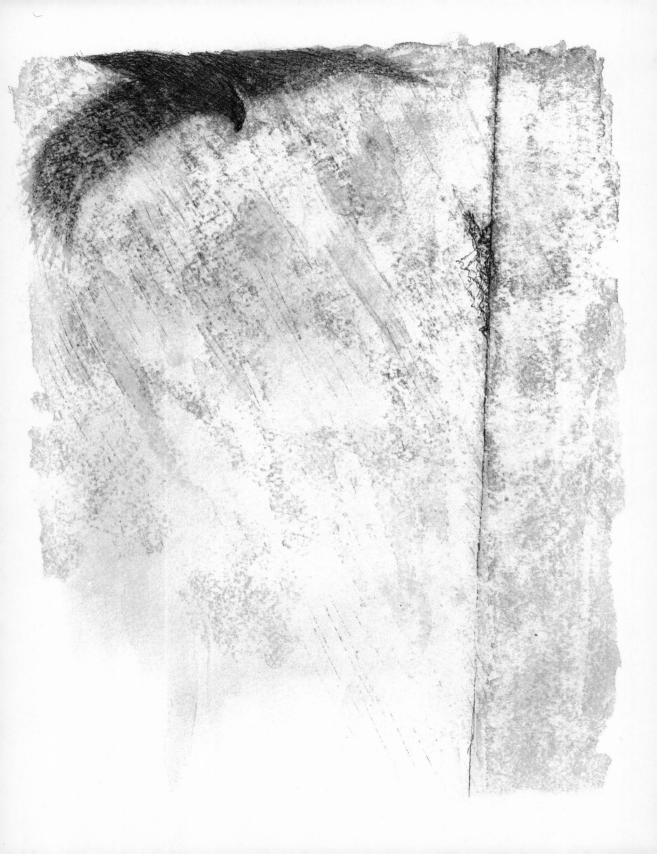

Shame held Solomon silent. The eagle flew far, far up, and disappeared in a tower that seemed to pierce the very sky.

Trembling with despair, King Solomon made one last, frantic effort to climb to a place where he might enter the castle. By now the thunderstorm had fully burst; the rain was falling heavily and steadily; the lightning flashed like a mocking eye, and the thunder crashed and threatened in his very ear.

The walls of the castle were running with water; he could get no hold on the slippery wet stone, whose gritty surface crumbled away in his hands. He was soaked to the skin, his garments were by now mere strips and shreds of silk. His palms bled, his beard was torn, his sandals hung in rags of leather from his burning feet. The weight of his crown seemed to draw a ring of fire around his head.

When he came to the window he had no more strength left. He sank back on the ledge, wiping his wet face with his soaked sleeve.

The sky above grew black as pitch. A third eagle

31

was spreading its wings high overhead, so that the whole of the sky was hidden. It was so old that hardly any feathers remained on its dark, broken skin; its huge, distant eyes were white with age and its cracked yellow beak seemed ready to drop off. King Solomon looked up, involuntarily shielding his face with his hands.

In a high shriek of anger the eagle spoke.

"The servants have left a speck of dust on the windowsill!" it cried. "I must brush it off with my wing." And it began to dab with its ragged wing feathers at the ledge where Solomon was clinging.

Shrinking back as close as he could to the wall, grasping the stone to steady himself, the King shouted desperately:

"I am not a speck of dust! I am a man—a man—a living man! Do not kill me!"

The moment the words left his lips he felt a door open behind his body. He fell back into the castle upon a pile of soft, yielding material, where he lay, breathing fast, with shut eyes.

III

King Solomon rested long in the pearly half-light, under the immense arch of the ceiling. At last his thoughts began to clear.

He opened his eyes and sat up.

The couch on which he rested was all of feathers, whose shining colors paled and glowed continually, as if alive. The floor and the far walls of the wide chamber were soft and of a ruffled white; the many-colored pillars grew downward, narrowing, out of the ceiling.

33

In each wall was a large, round window, strangely tinted, and the light came through in throbs of subdued and changing hues.

Wondering, Solomon arose and moved down the hall. His mind passed from his strange surroundings to the events that had brought him here. Holding together his torn, soaked garments, he exclaimed in a burst of anger:

"I see it now! Benaiah was right! Ah, Ashmodai, King of the Demons, you have tried once more to harm me and bring me to distress. But wait. I shall conquer and punish you yet! With the help of—of—"

Of whom? In vain did the Great King struggle with his memory; the Name was not in his mind. Again he sank into bewilderment. Surely Ashmodai could not have caused him to forget the Name! No, this trouble of his was not the doing of the Demon King.

But how, then, had it happened? How could he, Solomon, son of David, the beloved singer of psalms, have forgotten? Never did it enter his mind that the

Name of God could not remain in the soul of a blas-
phemer.

A broad flight of stairs interrupted the King's pac-
ing. To his distress, Solomon saw that the staircase
was of frightful depth. Down and down forever, like
a fan perpetually drawing out, went the soft, feathery-
white steps.

"No," thought the King, "it is bad enough where
I am. I shall not try to descend this endless flight. It
may reach down into the center of the earth for all
that I can tell."

But as he gazed, leaning his head too low, his
golden crown slipped off and went rolling over the
steps. It glided without a sound down and down the
feathery stairs. Soon to King Solomon's alarmed eyes
it was no larger than a bracelet, then no larger than a
ring, then just a golden sparkle in the bluish depths.
At last it was gone from sight.

The King pressed his hands to his brows in horror.
In this crown of his were jewels rarer than any others
in the whole world—jewels that had been brought as

tribute by water spirits from the caves at the bottom of the sea, gems that had been snatched by angels from strange fires. There were emeralds engraved with mystic signs which gave the Great King superhuman powers over demons and beasts. And now this crown, the envy of all the kings in the world, was rolling away from him, perhaps to be lost forever! Before he realized it, King Solomon was hurrying down the endless staircase after his crown.

Holding on to the slippery balustrade and running with all the speed of his weary limbs, Solomon at last caught up sufficiently to keep the crown in sight, a faint golden glitter always vanishing in the depths. With all his efforts he could come no closer to it. Just as he was about to give up in despair, the crown stopped at a landing, and he saw it roll through the first of three curious doors, which opened upward and outward like a spreading wing and then sank down again.

King Solomon hesitated outside the door, wondering how he could make it open for him. But as he

approached, the door slowly rose of itself, and he passed under it.

No sooner had it shut down behind him than Solomon started backward in amazement.

Before him was a busy street, full of hurrying people. By the pillars at the corner and the curve of the deep-rutted road, he recognized it as one of the principal streets in his own city of Jerusalem! He stepped forward with a glad exclamation and waved his arm to the people. But no one stopped or even turned a head. He ran out into the middle of the road, where donkeys and litters were rapidly crisscrossing, and raising his hand, commanded the people to stop. Even as he stood there, a litter with yellow curtains, whose shafts were carried by four barelegged Arabs, came upon him, and before he could jump aside, passed right through him!

Bewildered, the King withdrew to the wall. He realized that he had become as a shadow and that no one saw him. People went on walking through him— now a couple of grave and leisurely merchants with wide-awake eyes, now a naughty, half-dressed street-boy running away from a cloth dealer whose linens he had trailed in the dust, now a veiled girl hastening home from the market.

A shout of children's laughter attracted his attention. Nearby, in a doorway, a crowd of urchins with smudged noses and plump brown cheeks were sitting. One of them, elevated on a stone, seemed to be adopting a position of superiority over the others; he held a stick in his hand and looked as stern as two large dimples and laughing eyes would let him. Before him, one boy was crouching low in pretended fear and another was standing straight and frowning boldly.

"Come," exclaimed a fourth boy, "speak up and tell the judge truly—did you take the money out of the oil jars this man claims he left with you?"

"No, I didn't," said the bold-faced lad.

"Yes, yes, he did!" whined the crouching fellow.

"Oh, be quiet!" exclaimed the pretended judge, throwing down his stick. "You don't know how to do this. Do you think they let people interrupt in

39

King Solomon's court? Wait for your turn." Picking up his stick again, he turned to the other boy.

"Prisoner," he declaimed, "this man says he left three hundred gold coins in three oil jars for you to take care of while he went away. When he came back you gave him three oil jars, but they were full of oil, not gold. Now your neighbors say you have suddenly got three hundred pieces of gold. I think you are guilty."

"Well, but King Solomon judged the other way," interrupted the prisoner.

"I don't care if he did," cried the "judge" heatedly. "I know what really happened. Take out your purse. And *you* are not supposed to talk!"

The supposed prisoner pretended to draw out a purse.

"Bring me some water." A pitcher, also imaginary, was offered.

"Now," went on the "judge," "drop the gold in the pitcher of water." The boys all leaned as if to see. "Look! The gold rises to the top, and it is covered

with drops of oil. This proves it used to be in the oil jar! Prisoner, you took the money!"

"Ah, how did you guess it?" jeered one of the boys.

"I heard my father say that if the King had tried this way, he would have found out who was right. And I know Rachmiel really did steal the money, because I play hide-and-seek in his cellar, and I *saw* him take the money out," stated the "judge" calmly. "But if anyone had tried to tell the King—ooh!— wouldn't he have got a whipping!" And the boys burst out laughing.

The King had watched the game to the end, biting his lip. Now he exclaimed angrily:

"Ah, you rascal! What if I made a mistake in such a trifling matter? My wisdom sees into the hearts of men, if not into their every deed. It is far more important to know a rogue from an honest man than to make every trifling judgment correctly!"

Stepping back indignantly, the King found himself passing under the door. The scene went out before his eyes like a blown candle flame; King Solomon was

alone in the twilight of the immense palace, facing
the three strange doorways.

A glittering along the snowy floor caught his eye;
it was his crown, rolling away to the door on the
right. But wait—was it surely *his* crown?

Its gems were dim and dull as glass, and its gold
was like tarnished brass. He hurried across the threshold, under the rising door, and stooping, almost had
his hand upon the crown when it gave a bound and
disappeared.

In the sudden sunlight the King blinked his eyes.

He was standing on the porch of a palace with
magnificent pillars and palms and marble steps. He
recognized it as belonging to Elmoni, the ambassador
of a powerful foreign king who had long resisted
Solomon's armies before he yielded at last to the
Great King.

From the cool inner courts came the slow padding
of an elephant's feet; the animal now came forward
and stood before the porch. It was a huge elephant,
pure white, covered with gold and silver trappings,

43

and it bore on its vast back a gorgeous purple-canopied gold howdah.

A slave, running beside the elephant, now struck its wrinkled, snowy side with a golden rod. It stopped short, the howdah swaying on its back. Then a man's arm, tinkling with heavy bracelets, reached out from its silken curtains and parted them. The man in the howdah looked out hastily, fearfully, waved his arm three times, then drew quickly back. The elephant lumbered on.

But Solomon had seen the man's face. With a shock of alarm, he recognized Amdiah. Amdiah was one of his most trusted servants, who took charge of Solomon's favorite son whenever the little boy went out to play. What was this man doing at the house of the King's enemy? He began to hurry after the elephant, but the animal's great paces and the speed of the silent slave, from whose soles the flesh had been cut that he might run faster, soon left the King far behind.

A dreadful fear stole into the heart of Solomon and would not be dismissed. Many times had the watchful

Benaiah warned his master against the craft of Amdiah, but the steady stern look of Amdiah's face and the affection he always showed the young prince had made the King laugh at Benaiah's suspicions. But what could a *faithful* servant be doing in the house of Elmoni, the ambassador of the King's enemy? And now, with a sinking feeling, the King recalled a remark he had heard Amdiah make: "Beware of the man who thinks he is a fool, for he is suspicious and watchful; but of the man who thinks himself wise, no one need beware."

Had Amdiah meant the remark for Solomon himself? The King clenched his fist at the thought of such insolence. But, after all, was it not true?

"Oh, if I could but get back to my palace!" groaned the King. "This very day they were to go hunting. Perhaps at this moment while I stand here helpless, he is doing harm to my son! Fool that I was—fool that I was!"

Beating his brow with his hands, the King walked back and forth in agony. In a moment he had stepped

46

back across the threshold and was again before the three doors in the silent, mysterious castle.

This time he did not wait for the crown to guide him. He eagerly went forward and pushed at the central door, which rose toward him and struggled against his body until he stepped aside and let it open freely.

Rushing in, he felt a fresh wind on his face. He was standing in a clearing of the forest. Down a thinly wooded slope a company of gay young people came streaming, all dressed in rich robes and shining with jewels. In front of them ran a tall boy of nearly ten years, with a narrow gold band in his ruddy hair.

Suddenly the boy pointed to a stag which had appeared in a clump of bushes not far off.

"Come," he cried to the youth who walked behind him, carrying a quiver of arrows and a small bow, "give me my weapons!"

As the young attendant detached an arrow from the quiver, the Great King, stepping forward, saw beyond doubt that the boy was his son. But although he

47

walked toward him and came in full view of the company, no one stopped, no one saluted him; even his son ran on without a glance of recognition. With a groan of helplessness Solomon stepped back; he was but a shadow.

The young prince hurried on ahead of all his attendants, who could hardly keep up with him. Now he turned around, his pretty face alight with eagerness, and laughed as he fitted his arrow to the bow.

"Get ready to shoot, all of you! I am sure that I alone will hit the stag. And if I do, you will know it is my arrow because it is tipped with gold." And he took careful aim.

At this moment Solomon perceived that Amdiah was among the attendants who followed the prince. He saw a quick, triumphant look vanish from Amdiah's cold face. Then he observed that Amdiah was standing so that the prince and the stag were in the same straight line before him. Amdiah was slyly taking aim, not at the stag, but at the young prince who so innocently turned his back.

49

A cry forced itself from Solomon's agonized lips; the sweat broke out on his brow.

He darted forward; hopelessly he placed himself between Amdiah and his beloved son; he knew he was a shadow and could not stop the arrow from reaching and killing the child.

"O God!" he burst out. "Protect him! I am but a powerless mortal, a weak and helpless speck of dust, full of vanities and foolishness. But Thou art great— Thou canst save and deliver! Let not my innocent child suffer for my errors—forgive me my crime against Thee that I compared myself to Thee. I confess my helplessness and my nothingness!" Sobbing, the King put his hands over his eyes that he might not witness the destruction of his child. . . .

The vision had been blotted out before he lifted his hands. He did not know what had happened in the forest, but the glory of the Holy Name lit up his heart with marvelous confidence and joy. How was it that he had suddenly remembered God? No matter; he had remembered. The blessing of the Spirit was with him, and he tremblingly hoped that he was pardoned.

A vast empty chamber stretched for miles before him. Weak and humbled, the King tottered aimlessly forward in the twilight. The silence quivered like a still forest of tall trees. Over his bent head he heard a many-winged fluttering; small, lovely child-faces glimmered about in the air. Then he heard the low, heartfelt singing of a voice, sweet and touching as the voice of David his father, repeating the confession:

"I am the Lord thy God, that giveth and taketh life . . .

"Thou shalt not take the Name of the Lord thy God in vain, for the Lord will not hold him guiltless that taketh His Name in vain. . . ."

Sobs shook the proud bosom of the Great King. Before him a parchment was held out by invisible hands; it was the Book of the Law. And before him also other hands held up his crown—his wonderful crown, bright with miraculous gems that gave power and wisdom.

But King Solomon did not look at the crown. He stretched out his hands toward the parchment and took it reverently by the borders and pressed it to his heart. . . .

In a rushing wind the palace walls separated and fell away; the floor was snatched from under his feet; he felt the sharp pressure of a huge beak against his body and heard the low, strong whirring of vast wings. Winds dashed by him with frightful force; he shut his dizzy eyes. . . .

Then the air was still and warm again; the fragrance of trees and flowers was about him; firm ground was under his feet. He opened his eyes hesitatingly.

Lo! There he stood in lovely, royal garments dripping with jewels like raindrops, beside his ivory couch heaped with silken cushions, on his marble terrace under the palm trees that overlooked the peaceful city of Jerusalem.

Before him stood Benaiah, captain of the guard, his hand nervously clasped upon his chain of yellow rubies, his face expressing the keenest anxiety and fear.

But the next moment, a gleam of joy made his face radiant. Stepping quickly forward, the captain fell on his knees and kissed the edge of the King's garment.

"All praise to thee, most wise and mighty King!" he exclaimed. "Thou hast chosen righteously, that thou didst not make use of that bewitched carpet."

The King raised Benaiah and embraced him, so glad was he to see him again.

"But I did make use of it, Benaiah, and it has brought me wisdom of a different kind," he said. "Why sayest thou that I did not use it?"

Benaiah gazed at the King in surprise.

"But, my lord, only one second—one moment of time—has passed since I saw the carpet vanish in the sky. Surely thou didst not have time to use it in that short moment."

"Moment?" The King drew a deep, gasping breath and stroked his curled beard. He was about to speak, but he was interrupted by the sound of shouting and cursing and the tramp of many feet hurrying up the steps that led to the terrace.

"Who comes there?" exclaimed the King.

Now the crowd burst into the terrace; in front was the young prince, who came running to his father and hid his face in the folds of the King's garments, trembling. Behind stood Amdiah, tightly bound with ropes, surrounded by the courtiers who attended the prince.

Scarcely stopping to salute the King, one of the courtiers began:

"Sire, to God alone be the thanks that our prince is saved! As we were about to shoot at a stag I observed that Amdiah was directing his arrow toward the person of the prince and not toward the stag. I leaped forward, intending if necessary to throw myself between them, but it was too late—the arrow had left the string.

"At that moment, when an instant's delay would have meant death, a hare started up in the ground between the very feet of the prince. He stumbled and fell on his face, and the arrow passed over his head."

The courtier ceased, breathless. The King stood

silent, patting the curly head that was pressed to his side. Then he looked up and his eyes were solemn and humble.

"Amdiah, I, the King, trusted you and believed in you. But God showed me in a vision that you were betraying me to my enemies. I saw that what I believed to be my understanding of men's hearts was naught but conceit, and my self-confidence naught but blasphemy. Glory to His Name, for He has enlightened me. Because you were His instrument, I will not slay you, but only banish you from my realms. Go!"

The bonds were loosed from Amdiah's arms; with sullen, downcast eyes he turned and walked slowly off. And the King buried his face in his hands and prayed.